ANGRY BIRDS™

Stella

POPPY'S PERFECT PRANK

←STELLA is the leader of the flock. She likes things done her way, but is always on the lookout for fun!

DAHLIA is the brains of the group! Is there anything she doesn't know? The quickest way to upset her is by disturbing her experiments.

WILLOW loves nature and is a true artist. She dreams big but is shy, and she often keeps her ideas inside her big striped hat.

POPPY is wild, funny and she loves practical jokes! The life and soul of the gang or a total goofball, depending on your mood ...

LUCA is the baby of the bunch. He thinks he's a bigger boy than he actually is, which sometimes lands him in trouble.

GALE used to be Stella's friend, but something changed ... She started thinking she's a princess and now bosses around a gang of minion pigs.

This diary belongs to:

≡ POPPY ≡

....

PRANKING QUEEN

OF THE ISLAND

4PM

'This is it! This is the best day EVER! This is going to be so TOTES FANTABULOUS that it'll go down in the *Book of Bird Records* as the prank to end all pranks. I'm so excited I can barely breathe, let alone speak. Seriously, Diary, it's going to be better than:

a) The time I swallowed twenty-seven of Dahlia's jet-propulsion sweets and whooshed around the island fourteen times in three minutes, which made Willow so dizzy she had to lie down for a day. Plus the smell was pretty spectacular, if you get my meaning. But it made ME laugh!

b) The time I put super-sticky tree sap on the swing so that Gale was stuck there for two hours. Which, if you think about it, was her own fault for trespassing. I don't know why

Willow was so annoyed. I mean, it could have been HER with her butt glued to a piece of rubber ... Though I suppose having Gale squawking outside your window might be a TEENSY-WEENSY bit annoying. But, still, worth it, right?

c) The time Stella wished we could live in a Winter Wonderland, so I spread super-slippery slime all over her treehouse to turn it into an ice rink, which it totally did! I mean, how was I to know that it would take so long to wear off that she'd be skidding around on her tail-feathers for a whole week?

d) And EVEN better than the time I hid inside Willow's hat and burst out just when she was getting to the crucial bit in her group portrait. OK, so it meant she had to turn Stella into a giant monster with two heads, and Dahlia looked more like one of the pigs, but it was still SOOO funny! At least me and Luca thought so.

Anyway, this time all the gang are just going to love it. In fact, they'll totes TWEET OUT LOUD, even if I do say so myself.

Right. Wish me luck, dear Diary. Not that I'm going to need it. I mean, I'm Poppy, Pranking Queen of the Island, the Prankster Extraordinaire herself. What could POSSIBLY go wrong?

POPPY, QUEEN OF PRANKS →

5PM

A lot, apparently. Like a HUMONGOUS lot. Like, imagine the most MAHOOSIVE thing you can possibly think of. And then quadruple it.

And that is still only HALF the amount of utter wrongness that just happened.

Oh, Diary, I can't even bring myself to tell you the details, but let's just say that a whole heap of things are a bit broken, Stella and Willow aren't speaking to each other, and Dahlia says I'm not allowed to even LOOK at her test tubes ever again in my entire life.

But, worst of all, I've been banned from pranking until next Sunday. That's, like, a whole week. Which is, like, FOREVER. I mean, how am I supposed to have any fun at all round here if I'm not thinking up even an itty-bitty little trick or two? Stella said they've put up with the pranks for long enough and it was about time I realised it's not ALL about me. I said I wasn't doing it for me, I was doing it for THEM. Only she pointed out that so far this month my pranks had left her with four missing spoons, a broken skateboard and a stain on the wall from where the pink flour bomb hit it that just WON'T wash off, so it wasn't really working out that well for her at all.

Plus Dahlia is tired of the endless racket, and how is she supposed to invent something as GENIUS as the wheel or sliced bread with a pain in the birdbrain? And Willow says that, even though she loves me more than the moon and stars themselves, I do 'have a tendency to ripple the biorhythms of the fragile island ecosystem with my desire for disturbance', which, like, I don't even UNDERSTAND. At least Luca thought it was funny! Though, to be fair, Luca thinks everything is funny.

I mean, I suppose Stella has a point. The pranks do sometimes, just SOMETIMES, have a habit of going a bit wrong. But, still, why couldn't Stella have just made me wash the dishes for a day, or fill in some pig holes, or have confiscated my drumsticks? Well, she confiscated those as well, but if she hadn't banned me from pranking I could probably have 'borrowed' something from Willow or Dahlia to use instead. I even said sorry a hundred-and-thirty-three times (Dahlia counted), but not even that was enough to change Stella's mind.

It's NOT FAIR. I mean, asking me not to prank is like asking Dahlia not to THINK or Stella not to SING or Willow not to do all the bazillion things Willow does. Or the pigs not to EAT or Gale not to LOOK IN THE MIRROR. Which, like, HELLO!

This is worse than the time I broke my cymbals and had to use two plastic plates instead, which do not have the same sound, no matter what Willow says.

AND the time I thought I'd lost Luca down the volcano after firing him from my slingshot and spent four hours looking for him (it turned out he'd flown straight over and was back in his treehouse playing pigs and ladders).

AND the time I ACCIDENTALLY exploded my own treehouse and had to share with Dahlia while she rebuilt it. Which wouldn't have been so bad except she TOTES talks in her sleep AND hogs the bed. I fell off twelve times and in the end I just slept inside the bass drum, which, to be fair, is where I've stayed ever since, but even so it was completely ANNOYING. Only not as annoying as today.

Today is, without doubt, the WORST DAY EVER. This is so HUMONGOUSLY AWFUL that I really think the WORLD IS ENDING. That, or it has to be a dream. Yes, that's it. There is no way that something this TOTES TRAGIC is actually happening to me. In fact, I'm going to go to bed right now and when I wake up tomorrow everything will be back to normal. And I, Poppy, the Queen of Pranksters, will be back to my usual tricks …

MONDAY

8AM

Sooooooo, the world doesn't seem to have *actually* ended. I mean, I'm still here for a start. Unless there was some kind of mega explosion, which catapulted me into a parallel universe where everything is EXACTLY THE SAME. Same old trees, same old sky, same old pigs building what looks like an upside-down helicopter ...

So, the only other possible explanation is that the entire PRANKTASTROPHE was nothing more than a figment of my imagination. Completely, utterly, definitely, no-doubt-about-it a DREAM.

Of course! It's all so obvious. Any minute now, I'm going to rush over to Stella's and she's going to think up some madcap scheme for us to trick those pigs into flying the helicopter in loop-the-loops until they're dizzy. And Dahlia will give me back my drumsticks, which she totally only borrowed to stir her latest creation, which, like, DUH! And then Willow will say we should all have a group hug and EVEN THOUGH Stella thinks that flappy-feely stuff is for feather-brains and hippy chickens she'll do it anyway and we'll all be BBFFs (Best Bird Friends Forever) again.

Yay!

Or, as Stella would say: GAME ON!

8.30AM

OK, so either I am still stuck in a REALLY bad dream in which Willow, Dahlia and Stella have been replaced by evil zombie birds who just keep rolling their eyes and turning their tails up at me. Or it wasn't a dream after all and I really *did* carry out the ULTIMATE PRANK, which really *did* go spectacularly, horribly, disastrously WRONG and I really *am* banned from pranking for SEVEN WHOLE DAYS.

Either way, it's a TOTAL NIGHTMARE.

At least I was right about something. It WAS the prank to END all pranks! Which would be SOOO FUNNY if it wasn't so TRAGIC.

Seriously, like, HOW am I going to get through this? I mean, I can't remember the last time I didn't carry out at least ONE prank a day. But Stella says one prank is one prank TOO MANY and I'm not even allowed a SINGLE trick until next SUNDAY because by then I should have learned my lesson! I said if she gave me the lesson super-quickly then we could get the whole thing over and done with and everybody would be happy again. Only she said that my attitude PROVED I didn't even have a clue what the lesson was and that was why I needed seven days to think about what I'd done. Errr … BORING!

More than that, it's IMPOSSIBLE.

Stella says there's no such thing as impossible and a girl can do ANYTHING she wants if she puts her birdbrain to it. But that's because no one has ever banned her from, like, wearing the colour PINK for a whole week or not blowing bubbles for FIVE MINUTES.

But don't let it be said that Poppy isn't up for a challenge. Oh no, I will TOTES surprise Stella by not getting bored for a whole day and then she'll HAVE to change her mind, won't she!

Won't she?

10AM

It's AMAZING how TOTES fascinating staring at a single twig on a tree for a WHOLE HOUR can be. For example, I can tell you it has seventeen leaves, and only one of them is orange, plus a ladybird has walked up and down it four times.

Like, WHAT IS THAT ABOUT? Seriously, what is the ladybird THINKING? Is it testing out the time it takes to get from one end to the other for some kind of bug building project? Or maybe it's sending out signals to alien ladybirds in outer space just by foot tapping. Or perhaps it's keeping fit, which I agree is, like, TOTES important. Personally, I stretch my tail feathers and do a little light Tai Chick every morning with Willow.

Only not today, obviously. So it will be ALL Willow's fault if I seize up and suffer BIRDBREAK!

Is that even a thing?

It should be.

See? Not bored ONE BIT. I am TOTES going to be able to do this!

12PM

OK, so the twig did get a TEENSY-WEENSY bit blah after the ladybird flew off. But I absolutely PROMISE, cross-my-heart-and-hope-to-fly that I am NOT BORED. I mean, what could POSSIBLY be boring about counting how many feathers I have (answer: three thousand, seven hundred and forty-nine), or how many tin cans I have in my collection (thirty-seven), or how many backwards somersaults you can watch Luca do before you feel sick (answer: not that many at all)? And next I'm going to REALLY liven things up by seeing how many cherries I can fit in my beak at once! Which is, like, TOTES FASCINATING or WHAT?

8... 9... 10...

2PM

Eleven! Which IS kind of fascinating if you think about it. Which, I have. For, like, a WHOLE TWO HOURS.

OK. So, I admit, it's getting an incey-wincey bit boring now. But what did they say in that business book that Dahlia found on the beach and made us all read, saying that we 'might learn something'? 'When the going gets tough, the TOUGH GET GOING'. And also 'THINK OUTSIDE THE BOX'. And do 'BLUE-SKY THINKING'. So I am really going to give it a hundred and ten per cent, think about blue skies outside a giant box and generally TOUGH IT OUT!

3PM

There is only so much thinking about blue skies you can do when you're not allowed to drop things out of them onto other birds or pigs. Or hide inside the box you're supposed to be thinking outside of and then burst out in a puff of smoke and shout 'SURPRISE!' Plus Dahlia says there is NO SUCH THING as 'giving a hundred and ten per cent' – it is mathematically IMPOSSIBLE, and she is going to possibly EXPLODE if I ever suggest it again.

If you ask me, it's mathematically IMPOSSIBILE that she hasn't ever actually exploded as she threatens to do it so often. Actually, I think Willow has begged her to cut down on explosions as they're environmentally unfriendly and ripple those biorhythms.

Anyway, the point is I'm BORED. And it's not even the end of DAY ONE yet. I'm just going to have to hope something PRANKALICIOUS happens without me to make life interesting.

4PM

Ooh, I think something's happening on the beach. The pigs seem to have got their upside-down helicopter, which is actually digging some kind of tunnel, stuck underground and it's making a massive CLANKING noise. This could be INTERESTING!

4.15PM

Or not. They just climbed off and went back to Gale's castle looking extra sheepish. I mean, where's the fun in THAT? They could at least have put it into reverse and rocketed backwards so that they all fell off into one of the swamps! It's a sorry day when not even the pigs are making a mess of everything.

5PM
Bored.

6PM
BORED.

7PM
TOTES BOREDAMUNDO.

8PM
A hundred and TWENTY per cent BORED!

Seriously, It's been ONE DAY of not pranking, but it feels like a HUNDRED YEARS! Or at least, I don't know, two days or something. And I know I've said this before but IT'S NOT FAIR. I didn't *mean* for it all to go horribly WRONG. I was only trying to be funny and now NO ONE likes me and I'm all on my OWN and I can't even drum properly to show just how DISASTROUS this is. I tried using some twigs instead of drumsticks but they snapped in SECONDS. Then I tried

Willow's knitting needles but she said if I
bent them then the scarf she was making for
someone as a present would be all wonky and I
wouldn't want that, would I? I said that, since it
was obviously not for ME, I didn't really CARE
two tweets.

Only that's not TRUE. Of course I care.
It's just that this no pranking business is
making me all cross and well, not ME. I just
don't feel like Poppy anymore. I feel like ...
Oh, hang on ... That can't be ... Only, it is ...
NOOO!!!... This must be how GALE feels most of
the time!

That's not good. That's not good AT ALL.

OK. Tomorrow is going to be better.
Tomorrow I'm going to find a new hobby that
doesn't involve making things slippery or
sticky, or bursting out of things, or breaking
ANYTHING at all.

I am going to be a whole new me. No one will
recognise me. I'll be Poppy Version 2.0.

No longer will I be Poppy the Prankster Extraordinaire; Poppy Pranktastic; Poppy, Princess of Prankers.

No, I'll just be plain old Poppy.

Or plain NEW Poppy, I should say.

9PM

Although, thinking about it, that does sound the TEENSIEST bit BORING, doesn't it.

9AM

Right. I am TOTES into this. Stella says only boring birds get bored and I, Poppy, am possibly the LEAST BORING bird on this island ...

Except Dahlia when she made an ice-cream machine out of two washed-up pram wheels, a bicycle helmet and an alarm clock.

Or Willow when she told that scary story about the Bad Prince and his Minion Frogs and it was so terrifying that we all stayed at Stella's for a sleep-over that night.

OR Stella when she dreamed up that scheme to turn the parasail into a giant trampoline and the pigs got on and boinged themselves into a nettle patch by mistake.

But still, the point is, I'm *sooo* not boring.

So I am a hundred per cent NOT going to be bored today. I just need to think up some new hobbies and it's GAME ON! I mean, how hard can that be?

1PM

OK. So maybe it was just a *leeettle* bit harder than I thought. I mean, it's been four hours and so far all I've come up with to stop me being bored is:

1. Become island solitaire champion.
2. Learn to play bongos.
3. Learn to do a triple forwards somersault with quadruple twist.
4. Bake cookies in interesting shapes.

Only I don't HAVE any bongos and I tried using buckets but the sound is just, well, plasticky.

Plus I don't even know how to play solitaire and the only person who does is Dahlia and she says she's FAR too busy with her groundbreaking scientific experiment for games.

And when I tried to do the somersault I overtwisted and flew right out of the treehouse and landed WHAM BAM on top of Willow who was meditating, which TOTES disturbed her biodoodahs. Plus I MAY have squished her raspberry and carrot muffin in the process and there is nothing yuckier than a squished muffin in the morning.

So then I tried baking cookies in the shape of all the girls and Luca so I could give one to each of them as a present, only something must have been wrong with the ingredients, because when they came out of the oven they didn't look like birds at all but more like wonky PIGS. Willow said they looked BEAUTIFUL, which was TOTES a nice thing to do, especially after the muffin disaster earlier. But then Stella got all ruffled because she thought Willow meant that she really DID look like an exploded pig so now they're not talking AGAIN and it's ALL MY FAULT. I just can't seem to do anything right at the moment.

Maybe trying to be a totally new me was a mistake. Maybe I should stick to what I know after all. Only all I know about is drumming and

pranking and I can't drum because I STILL can't find anything to use as drumsticks and I can't prank or I'll be banished to live in the castle with Gale or WORSE.

Not that I can think of anything worse.

2PM

Oh, wait, I just thought of something: WHAT IF you got turned invisible. I mean it SOUNDS prankalicious. Because you could TOTES hide in Gale's castle and pretend to be a ghost bird. Or listen in on her top-secret conversations and find out what she and the pigs are planning next. OR sneak her crown away without anyone noticing, and try it on for yourself. Not that I'd do that, OBVS. Because that would be stealing.

Only the thing about being invisible is that no one would be able to see you. And so maybe they'd just forget about you altogether, and you'd be all on your lonesome FOREVER. Plus, if there's one thing I've learned from Stella it's

that girls should be SEEN AND HEARD AT ALL
TIMES.

3PM

And another thing: Playing kiss chase with the
pigs. I mean, UGH. Boys are just so, I don't
know ... weird? At least the PIGS really are.
ESPECIALLY Handsome Pig. I mean, for a
start he's TOTES in love with Gale. Which, like,
HELLO? Plus he thinks he's the best-looking pig
in the world. But THAT'S not saying much, is it!

HELLO GORGEOUS!

Girl friends are just *sooo* much more fun. Or, at least they are when you haven't pranked them into a MEGA sulk.

I tell you something though, Diary. The day you catch me kissing a boy is the day the world really will END.

5PM

World's End would be a good name for a band though.

OOOH! That's what I'll do. I'll form a new band. Me and ... hmmmm ... I need to think of someone.

5.15PM

The pigs? No. They'd just fall off the stage. Plus Handsome Pig would TOTES try to hog the limelight.

5.30PM

Or ... maybe ... just me and Luca. We could be a double act. Only not called World's End because

that is just mega gloomy but The
Rhythm Twins! Only we're
not that twinnish.
So maybe Little
and Large! Or,
wait, I've got it:
Birds Aloud!!

   That's IT! I'm a genius after all. I'm TOTES
going to form a band with Luca and it'll be
fabuloso and Stella will be SO jealous that she'll
beg to join and before you know it the girls will
all be back together again.

7PM
Soooooo, that didn't go as well as I hoped. Willow
got annoyed with Luca singing so loudly and

told him he should play the pan pipes instead. Only Luca got annoyed with the pan pipes because some of them are still blocked with pebbles from the time I pranked Willow to make her think she'd lost her hearing (which was hilarious, although possibly not for Willow who is always AT ONE with nature that she says she can practically here the grass growing. And for a minute she thought her life had gone TOTES out of tune). Anyway, Luca wandered off and the next thing I knew I was a solo act. AGAIN.

I am SO tired of being on my own. It's like I said before: being invisible gets lonely after a while. And I KNOW I'm not REALLY invisible. But that's what not pranking feels like. And not hanging out with your Best Bird Friends.

8PM

Maybe that's where I'm going wrong. I mean, I'm TRYING to be different. I'm TRYING to mend my pranking ways and be less ... Poppyish. Only I've been TRYING to do it all on my OWN.

When really what I need is a good teacher. And who better to learn from than my home birds?

I mean, there's Stella who's DEFO the best leader of the flock a bird could ask for. She's sassy. She's smart. She never gives up. And, OK, so she won't EVER admit she's wrong (which she TOTALLY is, at least SOME of the time), but there's no bird I'd sooner rely on in a crisis, or call on when I need some good old-fashioned FUN!

There's Dahlia who's preppy, practical, and a total Bird Brain (and I mean that in the best possible way).

Because who else can conjure up a working hovercraft from an airbed, a kazoo and some plastic forks? I mean, she's the best scientist on the entire island.

OK, so she's the ONLY scientist on the entire island. But even if the science champion of the whole universe moved in next door, Dahlia would STILL be the best. At least to me.

Then there's wonderful Willow. She may be a total hippy chick, and the group hug thing can be a TEENSY-WEENSY bit annoying after the seven-BAZILLIONTH time. But she's artistic. She's sensitive. And, most of all, she's QUIET. Which I admit, is TOTES NOT my strong point, so there's LOADS I can learn from her.

Even Baby Bird Luca could teach me a thing or two. Say if I ever needed to know how to imitate Stella, or Gale, or a pig getting stuck in a paper bag and walking into a wall.

Which, I think it's safe to say, I don't. At least not right now. What I really need is to learn how to be less ... LOUD.

And how to CHILL.

And how to ALWAYS think of others before myself, even if it's a tiny ant or a beetle or even a flea.

And maybe even how to do my feathers in natty dreads.

OK, possibly not the last one but TOTES all the others.

So, starting tomorrow, I am going to kiss goodbye to Poppy and wave hello to WILLOW THE SECOND!

And I'm determined to be the best pupil ever. I'm going to hang on her every tweet and follow her every bounce.

By the end of the day I'll probably be chatting to the chrysanthemums and dancing with the dandelions.

I can hardly wait!

7AM

Oh, I'm so TOTES excited. Today's the day I get rid of my Poppy-ness and start chilling like Willow. By teatime I will be as calm as a cucumber. Or is it cool as a cucumber? Oh, WHATEVER, I am going to be cucumber-like anyway.

Though why anyone would want to be green and knobbly I have NO IDEA. Maybe I'll ask Willow when I go to hang out in her treehouse.

But first I am going to MEDITATE, because Willow says it's the best way to start the day i.e. by getting in tune with the island's biothingummyjigs, which is like SUPER-important apparently. All I need to do is say OM a bit and empty my mind. I mean, how hard can THAT be?

MEDITATING CUCUMBER ⟹

7.15AM

Hmm. Quite hard as it turns out.

Meditating is NOT AT ALL as calming as Willow claims. For a start all that OMMING is buzzy and makes my beak tingle, which is TOTES distracting. Plus emptying your mind is easier said than done. I mean, I tried SUPER-hard to concentrate on NOTHING. But then almost immediately I thought, 'what does NOTHING look like? Is it see-through like air? Or is it dark like a black hole?' And then stuff kept wandering into the nothing, like Dahlia getting all scientific and doing some crazy experiment on NOTHING, and the pigs trying to

41

dig a hole in NOTHING, and Willow getting her feathers in a twist because they were destroying NOTHING.

And then before I knew it there was a full-scale FLAP going on in my head and all over NOTHING. Seriously, meditation makes rocket science look EASY-PEASY if you ask me. Not that I've tried it, because Dahlia won't let me. But it can't be ANY harder, that's for double sure.

Unless … maybe the reason I'm getting it wrong is because I'm still too, well, Poppyish. Maybe all that loud drumming means I can't hear the universe BREATHE or whatever it is I'm supposed to be doing. Maybe I'm not ready for this much chilling yet. I mean, you don't learn to forward flip by jumping off the edge of a CLIFF.

OK, well, maybe I did try that. But only the once.

No, what I need is proper lessons first. I need to be taught to TAKE IT EASY, to TUNE IN to the environment, to TREAT my body like a TEMPLE. And other things beginning with T. And the only way I'm going to learn to do any of that is by getting it straight from the bird's beak i.e. Willow. Let's just hope I don't disturb her own bio-oojamaflips when I land on her doorstep with my dawn chorus!

10AM

OK, this is what I've learned so far:

1. That 7.23 is WAY too early to wake Willow when she's been up until silly-o'clock trying to put the final touches to a painting of what looks like a giant pool of custard in some jam, but which she says is ACTUALLY sunrise over the mountains and is a celebration of Mother Nature, new life, and also something called the summer solstice. Which it turns out is NOT some kind of medicine but when the sun is at its highest point in the sky. Which, like WHO KNEW? Well, Willow. And now me. So, like, yay me!
2. That you're supposed to visualise an empty room when meditating.

3. That asking questions whilst meditating is SO NOT cool, or calm, or cucumber-like. Only I TOTES needed to know whether my OM was too high and how big the room was that I was supposed to be visualising. Like, ballroom-size or bathroom-size? And what colour are the walls?

4. That a) Yes, my OM was WAY too high and only dogs and dolphins would be able to hear it, which I thought sounded good, but which Willow said is so NOT the point and b) it 'doesn't MATTER what size the room is or what colour the walls are, but for nirvana's sake will you PLEASE STOP TALKING POPPY!'

Which, I like, TOTES tried to do only, it turns out that being QUIET is even harder than OMMING. Seriously, I don't know HOW Willow manages it.

She says she lets her thoughts 'speak silently in her head'. Only what is the point of that when there is one of your BBFFs right there next to you to fess all your thoughts to instead of keeping them caged in? Willow said if it *really* mattered, like if something was at stake, like the life of a PRECIOUS BUTTERFLY then I would be able to keep quiet. I just need to use WILLPOWER. So I asked if I could find some willpower at the beach maybe, which was totally meant to be a joke but she gave me one of her looks, and we all know how scary THAT can be.

Anyway, she had a BRILLIANT idea, which is that I'm going to do a sponsored silence. So, for every minute I don't say a word, she, Stella and Dahlia will devote an extra FIVE minutes to cleaning the common area. Willow says that way everyone wins. Stella said she wasn't sure that cleaning was that spectacular a prize, and couldn't it be candy cake pops instead? Then Dahlia said I'd only manage a few seconds anyway so there wouldn't be much of a prize whatever it was. Which TOTES ruffled Willow's feathers because she said they should have more faith in their friend i.e. me. Er, YEAH.

So, I am TOTES going to do this silence thing, and for a whole HOUR, which will mean … um … a LOT of cleaning for Stella and co.

And I'm starting right NOW …

10.01AM
Haven't said a word yet.

10.02AM
Or yet.

10.03AM
Or yet. Although Stella said writing in my diary was cheating and Dahlia said it wasn't and Stella said it was and Willow said maybe they should all be doing sponsored silences, which shut them up anyway.

10.04AM
Oh, I've just thought of a joke. A TOTES brilliant one with a banana, a balloon and Handsome Pig's underpants. Only I won't say it yet. I will

SAVE it for ... fifty-six minutes' time when I'm allowed to speak again.

10.05AM

It is VERY funny though.
Like funnier than: 'Why
don't sharks eat clownfish?'
(Answer: because they taste
funny. Geddit?!)

10.06AM

And EVEN funnier than: 'What's yellow and dangerous?' (Answer: shark-infested custard!)

10.07AM

Oh, this is TORTURE. It's like having an itch, and you just NEED to scratch it ... I'm not sure I can keep it INSIDE any more ...

10.30AM

OK, so the sponsored silence wasn't a complete success. Which is TOTES not my fault. When you think about it, if it's anybody's fault, it's Willow's for not letting me go and find some willpower before I started. On the other hand, the joke DID make everyone laugh. Which was kind of nice as it's been a while since I've done that. Only I'm not supposed to be making people laugh, because that's what POPPY does and I don't want to BE Poppy any more, do I? Willow said I was thinking about it all wrong and that I shouldn't be trying to be someone else. What I should be doing is concentrating on all the things that are SPECIAL about being Poppy. But, other than pranking and drumming, what is there? Willow said she was sure I could think of some more things that make me unique. But I told her I TOTES couldn't, and it's probably because I got left off the list for good stuff like that when I hatched, along with willpower. Willow tried to give me one of her hugs then, only my feathers were so ruffled she couldn't get close enough and in the end she said maybe I should try knitting instead, or weaving, or making pictures out of sea-shells. Only I said I'd rather go back to the empty room thing. ON MY OWN.

Only that's TOTES not true. The point was to learn from my friends instead of doing it all by myself.

11AM

Hang on. Maybe that's it. Maybe the problem isn't me after all. Maybe it's WILLOW. Maybe it's that I picked the wrong friend to learn from. After all, me and Willow couldn't be more different. We are so NOT peas-in-a-poddish. We're like a pea and a carrot.

Or chalk and cheese.

Or cheese and chocolate. (Obviously I'm the chocolate!)

I mean, if you get your lessons wrong, it's OBVS not your fault but your teacher's, right? So I'm getting a new teacher. One with the biggest bird brain on this island. That way, I absolutely, TOTES cannot fail.

I will learn to be SERIOUS about SCIENCE.

I will learn to use LONG and STRANGE WORDS like "electromagnetism" and "antimatter" and "antidisestablishmentarianism".

And I will learn what they mean.

Most of all I will learn to STOP being SILLY. And DESIST from DRUMMING when I should be DECELERATING my NANOPARTICLES. Or something that I haven't just made up.

And I know JUST the bird who will make this happen.

1PM

Dahlia said she is definitely NOT the bird to make this happen right now as she is in the middle of a GROUNDBREAKING experiment to turn an old tyre into a hydrofoil, but if I go back at two o'clock then she will show me how to get electricity out of a potato. I said I hope she hadn't told Willow about stealing the potato's electricity because potatoes are livings things too with feelings and bioshenanigans. Only apparently these aren't as important to Dahlia as scientific progress is. That's what I think too, which is why I just KNOW this is going to work. Or at least I do now that I am about to become all BRAINY. Just think, by the end of this afternoon I could TOTES be PROFESSOR POPPY, with a white coat and glasses and a beard!

PROFESSOR POPPY!

OK, not a beard. Because that's just WAY old-fashioned to think all scientists are boys. Look at Dahlia, for a start.

1.30PM
Just had a thought. Imagine Dahlia with a beard! Now THAT would be hilarious! Maybe I could find a way to prank one onto her …

1.45PM
OH! That wasn't a good start. This is why I need Dahlia's help: so that she can STOP all this POPPY stuff that keeps pinging around in my head when I'm not concentrating and fill my brain with atoms and string theory and quarks instead. Quarks sound cute. Maybe they're like tiny little rabbits or squirrels. I hope so.

1.50PM
Though, more worryingly, what is string theory? I mean, string is string, right? Why does it even NEED a theory?

1.55PM

OK, I am off to find the answer to this, as well as:

a) Why is the sky blue?

b) What's at the end of the universe?

c) Which came first, the bird or the egg?
   And, MORE IMPORTANTLY ...

d) Do I, Poppy, have what it takes to be the next Eggbert Einstein, or ... whoever invented fake dog poo, fart sweets and itching powder?

6PM

Answers:

a) It isn't, we just see it that way because of wavelengths and something else I can't remember.

b) The universe doesn't end, it is INFINITE. Which means it goes on FOREVER. Which is totally mind-bending and I had to sit down for five minutes after thinking about it.

c) 'Seriously, Poppy? Are you EVEN going
   to waste a single BREATH on that dumb
   question?'
d) An absolute, definite, no-two-ways-about-it
   NO!

Which, like, I KNOW! TOTES unbelievable,
RIGHT? I mean, I've been back on my perch for
an entire FIVE MINUTES and I still can't get
my birdbrain round it. It seemed to be going so
well. I can remember it word for word:
   ME: DAHLIA! I'm HERE!
   DAHLIA: (dropping test-tube, which crashes
to floor) Like, thanks. No, really. Because I totally
needed a shock like that.
   ME: Phew. That's TOTES OK then. What was it
anyway?
   DAHLIA: Oh, only a love potion that could
have changed the course of history by making
Gale fall for Handsome Pig and forget all about
the stuck-up spoiled princess stuff because she's

way too busy reading poetry and listening to smoochy songs and stuff.

ME: Why does anyone even DO that? They, like, TOTES forget about all the other important stuff in life and go all gooey and weird. Love is crazy. I am SO never falling in love.

DAHLIA: I guess neither is Gale. Not now four months' work is all over the floor.

ME: But you've got, like a BAZILLION other experiments anyway. I mean look at all those pretty bottles. (Seriously, there are shelves and shelves of them: tall ones, fat ones, green ones, pink ones, fizzy ones, ones with a skull and crossbones on, which I guess is something to do with pirates. Though I have NO idea why as we TOTES haven't got any of those around here.)

DAHLIA: Seriously, Poppy. Don't touch those. In fact, don't even think about touching them. No, wait, don't even look at them or I might actually explode.

ME: But that's impossible. Even I know that spontaneous combustion is TOTES not real.

Plus HOW am I meant to not look at them? They're EVERYWHERE. It's like saying to Willow, 'Look, Wills, there's the most amazing rainbow over there but you absolutely cannot, not in a million years, not EVEN if the biodoodahs of the entire universe depended on it, look at it.'

DAHLIA: No, it isn't like that.

ME: Totes is.

DAHLIA: Totes isn't. Oh. Ugh. I just said 'totes'. And you know how much I totes don't like that.

ME: Totes.

DAHLIA: Seriously, stop it now.

ME: FINE. Only why does everything have to be 'seriously'?

DAHLIA: Because science is serious.

ME: Turning a potato into a battery doesn't sound very serious. I mean, you couldn't stick potatoes in your radio, could you. Well, you could, only they'd go soggy and end up smelling. Which, like EWWWW.

DAHLIA: This is going to be harder than I thought.

ME: What is? The experiment? Only it sounded so EASY-PEASY. I mean, if it's that hard, maybe we should start with something else. Something I absolutely cannot get wrong. Because, you know, it didn't go so well with the visualising thing earlier and I've TOTES learned my lesson from that. At least I think I have. What was it again? OOOOH, what's that thing? (The thing is a machine with lights that flash and something that goes ping and a sort of long nozzle on it and wheels so you can pull it along the floor.)

DAHLIA: That ... is the Prank Detector 5000.

ME: OOOHHH! That sounds AWESOME and EPIC all at once. What does it do?

DAHLIA: Er, the clue is in the name.

ME: 'Prank. Detector. 5000.' Hmmm. Oh, wait ... does it ... detect ... PRANKS?

DAHLIA: (sighs) Bingo.

ME: Like, if I'm thinking of a prank, it can tell?

DAHLIA: Again, bingo.

ME: Well, it's a good job I'm not even THINKING about thinking about a prank then, isn't it.

DAHLIA: Aren't you?

ME: Nope. Not even one bit. In fact, I'm not even *thinking* about thinking about thinking about a prank.

DAHLIA: I think you are.

ME: TOTES Am not.

DAHLIA: Well, the machine is flashing amber, which is your basic first-level warning that you're probably thinking about thinking about a prank.

ME: What happens if it KNOWS I am thinking about thinking about a prank. Or even just thinking about a prank. Or, actually PRANKING?

DAHLIA: Well, if you're definitely thinking about thinking about a prank it would flash red. If you were thinking about a prank, then the pings would get really fast. And if you were actually doing a prank then a warning siren would sound, telling you to step away from the slime or the goo or the gloop or whatever else it was you were busy tricking one of us with.

ME: As if I'd EVER do that.

DAHLIA: You did it last Friday, actually.

ME: Oh yeah. I so DID, didn't I! That was funny ... Well, maybe not when you had to wash all that gloop off the walls. But, I am SO over that. I'm a new bird. Or at least I'm getting there. I'm not even thinking about thinking about thinking about thinking about thinking about pranking ... How many thinks is that?

DAHLIA: Five. And if you're so sure, maybe we should test you.

ME: GAME ON!

DAHLIA: This isn't a game. It's serious.

ME: Like, OBVS. I knew that.

And so then Dahlia stuck the end of the nozzle on my head and pressed a button and the machine was still only on amber and pinging normally. But then, it was like thinking about nothing again. Because however hard I tried NOT to think about thinking about pranking, ideas for pranks kept popping into my head. Like, PING. There was a prank involving a catapult and a lime jelly. PING. There was another one with the potato battery and an

PING

PING

PING

electric shock. And then this whole CATALOGUE of pranks was piling up in my head, and the machine was PINGING like crazy, and the red light was flashing, and I figured it might be time to step away from the machine. Only before I got the chance, it made this MASSIVE grindy noise, and actual SMOKE started coming out of the nozzle and the whole thing shot across the floor and out the door, just missing Stella and Willow who were coming to see what all the PINGING was about, before crashing into tiny little pieces on the forest floor, which made Willow wail in case it had landed on a ladybird. Which it hadn't.

So now everyone is super-mad at me AGAIN and I wasn't actually doing ANYTHING wrong. Which is TOTES not fair!

Plus there's still THREE whole days to go before I'm allowed to prank again.

Seriously, I am giving up. Tomorrow I'm not even going to get out of bed. Or the next day. Or the day after that. In fact, I may never get out of bed again AT ALL.

Then they'll be sorry.

Then they'll be begging me to think about just one TEENSY-WEENSY prank.

Won't they?

THURSDAY

7AM
Not getting up.

12PM
Not getting up.

5PM
STILL not getting up.

8PM
Going to bed i.e. Not moving because I am already in bed because I didn't get up and I am NOT GETTING UP tomorrow either.

So there.

7AM

Not getting up.

8AM

Not getting up.

9AM

Not getting up. Even though I am actually starting to think my body might have stopped working.

10AM

STILL not getting up.

EVEN THOUGH the others have gone off to the waterfalls to test out Dahlia's new wave-riding tennis-racquet bird-board.

And EVEN THOUGH I know it would be TOTES hilarious even if we all bounced off and ended up having an accidental bird bath.

And EVEN THOUGH they've packed a picnic and the instruments and it sounds like possibly the best day out, like, EVER.

Willow said the gang would be all unbalanced without me there.

And Stella said I was sulking more spectacularly than Gale, which, like, UGH. That is way harsh.

And Dahlia said well I had better not even THINK about pranking. So I said 'AS IF!' And she said 'Joke, Pops'. Which, now I'm thinking about it, maybe it was. Although it's kind of hard to tell with Dahlia sometimes. I mean, she can TOTES say the most hilarious gag without even cracking a smile. Like the time Gale got trapped in one of the pigs' crazy digging machines and, when they pulled her out, half her tail was left behind! Which, like, I KNOW! And Gale went LOOP-THE-LOOP crazy and squawked until she was blue in the beak, and Dahlia said, 'Keep your feathers on, Gale', and it turns out it WAS a joke, only Gale did NOT see the funny side. And nor did I until Dahlia explained it to me later.

But that's NOT the point. The point is I am so NOT going to prank. Because I'm going to stay RIGHT HERE IN BED where there is absolutely no one to prank, and nothing to prank with.

10.15AM

Except for the seventeen bottles that got washed up on the beach and I've been saving for a rainy day. Because they would be PERFECT to put messages in and pretend they're from Gale's DREAM BIRD who I'd tell her was, like, trapped on another island and she would TOTES try to save him, even though I made him up!

10.30AM

And for the twenty-two forks that I've collected
and was going to hang on a tree to pretend that
a new breed of cutlery plant had grown in the
night.

10.45PM

And the seventy-four assorted bits of rope, tins,
and wood that I actually have no idea what to
do with yet, but that doesn't mean I won't think
of something TOTES PRANKTASTIC to use
them for. I just need one of Dahlia's light-bulb
moments. And soon, because I tripped over the
tins collection fourteen times yesterday and
Stella got tangled in some rope and it took an
hour to disentangle her and she said it was about
time I gave the treehouse a sort-out. I said it
WAS sorted. I mean, I know exactly how many
bottle tops I have (eighty-nine). Only she just
sighed and said sometimes she thought I was
another species, rather than an actual bird.

11AM

Only thinking about it, maybe she had a point.

NOT that I'm not a bird, OBVS. Because what ELSE would I be? Some kind of feathered PIG?

No, I mean about the sorting out. Maybe I'll just get out of bed and have a quick tidy. After all, it'll help with the not pranking. And I can give all the stuff I don't need anymore to the others. Dahlia's always after more bits and bobs for her inventions. And Stella would ♡ that mirror I found. And Willow can have all the forks and make them into some kind of weird art thingy that tinkles in the wind and is in tune with biobajiminies and she'll be the happiest bird on the island.

OMG. I am TOTES brilliant after all!

4PM

I was wrong.

I'm not brilliant.

I'm a GENIUS!

An utterly, completely, absolutely
HUMONGOUS GENIUS.

Not only have I:

1. Got the tidiest treehouse on the entire island, like, EVER.

2. Given away seventeen plastic bottles, twenty-two forks, and seventy-four assorted bits of rope, tins and wood AS WELL AS two bouncy balls, three wonky wheels and something I thought was a kind of slide guitar only it turns out is an egg slicer, which, like WHAT IS THAT ABOUT?

3. Found one of my spare drumsticks and a piece of chewing gum I saved three months ago and it STILL tastes minty!

But I, POPPY THE MAGNIFICENT, have come up with a plan so PERFECT, so fantabulously PRANK-PROOF that I will be back in everyone's good books before you can say 'she sells seashells on the seashore'.

Or at least by teatime. Because, when I was leaving all my presents on the girls' perches, I had this utter BRAINWAVE. Like, wouldn't it be COOLAMUNDO if I cleaned their houses as well? So that when they get back from the waterfalls they won't even recognise where they live and they'll be SO grateful that they'll forget ALL about the pranking ban and everything will be exactly the way it was before. Only BETTER.

So I HAVE!

I've washed all of Willow's brushes and poured all the tiny bits of paint left in the old jars into one big jar because she is always saying stuff like 'Waste not, want not' so I TOTES didn't WANT

to WASTE any of it, even though it is all a bit of a
sludgy brown colour.

And I've tidied up Dahlia's laboratory so that
all the bottles are grouped according to colour
and then ranked in order of height. Which was
totally harder than I thought because she has
about a BAZILLION of them in there including
something called 'Hubble Bubble Double
Trouble', which I had to test (wouldn't you?)
so I poured a TEENSY-WEENSY bit of it on a
hazelnut and then there's this massive puff of
smoke and then PING the hazelnut turns into
TWO hazelnuts. Which like, I KNOW. Only I'm
not so keen on hazelnuts as they get gummed in

my beak, plus one of them was a bit small and mouldy, so I threw them both away. But still, good to know you can make more of stuff. Like drumsticks, maybe. Or milkshakes. Or even ME!

Except, no, because that would be a prank. Which I am TOTES not interested in because I have TURNED OVER A NEW LEAF and become RESPONSIBLE and SELFLESS, which is what Willow is always going on about, along with the biobazingas.

Oh, and there was this other bottle that kept changing from blue to pink and so I TOTES couldn't decided where to put it. Only in the end it was kind of decided for me because it fell into a bucket of paint and turned pink, which is when I had my next GENIUS idea. Because, the thing is, Stella's place is so spick and span already, there was no point just tidying it, so, instead I've given her whole HOUSE a new coat of paint, and not just any paint but PINK PAINT, which is guaranteed to send her SPINNING with happiness. Sometimes I am so brilliant I even amaze myself! Now all I have to do is relax and wait for the girls to get back and RAVE over their swanky new pads and tell me just how AWESOME I am and that they never doubted it in the first place.

EASY-PEASY LEMON-SQUEEZY.

5PM

Am I DOOMED?

Am I CURSED?

Has some EVIL NEMESIS been sitting in their underground volcanic lair for the last few days and plotting to RUIN MY LIFE?!

Because that is TOTES what it feels like!

I thought this time I had got it totally worked out. That the girls would come back and be so dizzy with delight that we'd all have a group hug and NOT EVEN STELLA would complain! Because she'd be so busy admiring the makeover and telling me I am her Best Bird Friend FOREVER.

Only what ACTUALLY happened went a little more like this:

1. Dahlia said I had ruined her entire bottle filing system and if I even THINK about sticking my beak one inch into her tree again she is going to actually, definitely explode. And I know she has said it before but this

time I think it might be true because I swear there was steam coming out of her head.

2. Willow went all white, then green, then purple and then hid inside her giant hat and refused to come out. Because it turns out those left-over paints WEREN'T left over at all– in fact she was about to use them all to finish her mural of 'the valley at peace'. I pointed out that at least I hadn't WASTED any and it's not my fault that she doesn't WANT them. Plus the brown is quite useful for doing mud, if you think about it and besides, the valley is very much NOT at peace anyway because ...

3. Stella is NOT spinning with happiness over her new paint job. Though she is totally spinning with something. Possibly RAGE. Because by the time she got back the paint had changed its mind and turned back to blue again and she so does NOT want a blue treehouse, it turns out. Or seventy-four assorted bits of rope, tins and wood on her floor. Or an egg slicer. Or the fork that I

turned into a useful peg but which she keeps bumping into and slightly spearing herself on. Plus ...

4. Luca accidentally fell into some wet paint and now he is changing colour every few seconds, which is pretty, but kind of weird.

So now I am back where I started: IN BED because Stella says she can't even speak to me until Willow has finished the emergency paint job to get rid of the blue, and Willow can't speak to me until Dahlia has helped her mix just the right shade of sunset pink again, and Dahlia can't speak to me because she's trying to catch Luca before he spatters anything and the entire island starts changing colour and makes us all feel seasick.

So I can't even tell them all I'm sorry. Which I TOTES am! I mean, I'm not sorry I tried to help, just that it all went an incey-wincey bit wrong.

I suppose I'll just have to say it in the morning. They're bound to have calmed down by then.

And if not, I'll have to think of a Plan B.

Like joining the CIRCUS.

Or emigrating to the OTHER SIDE OF THE WORLD.

Or moving in with GALE.

8PM

OK, maybe not the last one. I mean, it would have to be the END OF THE WORLD before that happened and this is only ALMOST the end. And the circus has too many bird-eating animals in it. But the other side of the world might be OK. Although knowing my luck it looks exactly like this side of the world and pranking is TOTES banned there too. In which case I might as well say sorry to Stella a bazillion times and be done with it.

8AM

So, I SAID I was sorry (a hundred-and-thirty-four times, not a bazillion, Dahlia counted, but still a LOT) and that I had only been trying to prove I was being responsible and had turned over a new leaf. Only Stella said all this proved was that even when I was deliberately NOT pranking I was so used to doing it that it somehow HAPPENED. And if I really wanted to do a good deed, then I could birdsit Luca for the day because he was getting on everyone's nerves. Plus his tailfeathers still can't decide what colour they want to be and it's giving her a headache.

So I said FINE. Because at least I'll be out of their way too so they can't find a single tiny thing to complain about. Plus the treehouse is looking TOTES empty after the tidy-up so I can pick up some new pieces from the beach.

And when I get back the day will nearly be over, which means NO PRANKING TIME will nearly be over. Which means I can start being the REAL Poppy all over again. The Poppy who plays drums LOUD and plays tricks even LOUDER. The Poppy who was one of the girls. The Poppy those girls used to ♡, even if I did sometimes get them into a bit of bother.

All I have to do is keep an eye on Luca.

Absolutely on Luca.

Not on anything else at all.

Not even if it's the most PRANKAMUNDO thing I have ever seen.

1PM

Oops.

Well, actually, DOUBLE oops.

Double oops with a CHERRY on top.

Double oops with a cherry, whipped cream, chocolate sauce, sprinkles AND those little silver ball things.

The thing is, I seem to have SLIGHTLY lost Luca.

I mean I only took my eye off him for a NANOSECOND. Or maybe ten seconds. Or possibly about ten MINUTES. But how was I to know that the pigs would be at the beach with their extendable nut-grabbers to poke around in treetops for whatever it is that Gale's after? Or that they would get stuck so the only way to reach them was to build this amazing LEANING TOWER OF PIGS? Or that they would TOTES wibble and wobble like JELLY before all falling into a massive heap of snouts and trotters on the sand?

Which was TOTES hilarious.

And TOTES when I realised Luca was GONE.

Which, like, I KNOW. I don't even want to think about how much trouble I'm going to be in this time. I actually think Stella might EXPLODE. Or get Dahlia to explode ME instead.

OMG. OMG. OMG.

OK that's not helping. If I'm going to think of a way out of this I need to calm down. I need to channel Willow.

That's it! I need to work out What Would Willow Do? She's bound to have the answer. OK, THINK, Poppy, THINK.

1.05PM

Have thought about What Willow Would Do. And I'm pretty sure Willow would go straight to Stella and fess up. Which is so NOT going to happen. Whatever I do, I know I absolutely cannot, under any circumstances, not even if pigs start to fly, tell Stella what I've done.

But unless I find Luca, then I'm going to absolutely have to do just THAT. Or explode myself. Which, like, no way. Willow was SO the wrong bird to pick. I need to try someone else. OK, I'm channelling Dahlia instead now. She's practical. She never lets pressure get to her. Plus she always follows rules and does everything in the right order because she says order is the FIRST RULE of science. Which is almost funny if you think about it. Which I'm totes not – I'm thinking about Luca and getting him back before someone turns my tailfeathers into a duster. And all I need to do is work out what's the first thing Dahlia would do ...

Put on protective glasses?

No that's so NOT going to help. Unless they were special X-ray vision glasses that could see into every nook and cranny on the ENTIRE ISLAND. Which is actually not a bad idea and I will totes ask her to invent some of those if she ever speaks to me again. But until then there is only one thing for it. I am going to have to look into every nook and cranny myself with my own, normal, non-X-ray eyes. That means the beach, the volcano, the waterfall, the woods, and (BIG

GULP) Gale's castle. But, Luca so WON'T be there, will he.

Will he?

2PM

OK. So, the thing is I have looked EVERYWHERE for Luca.

And he's NOT on the beach trying to bury himself in the sand.

And he's NOT in the volcano trying to see how far down he can get before his tailfeathers get burned.

And he's NOT whizzing down the waterfalls trying to break the world record for white-water rafting on a bottle-top.

And he's NOT in the forest trying to trick the pigs and I've tried calling and calling but he's not answering or even trying to imitate me which means he must be some place where he can't hear me.

And the only place far away enough, and with walls thick enough to block out MY voice AND

Luca's hearing is (BIG GULP NUMBER TWO) ... GALE'S CASTLE. Which, like I KNOW. I mean, could it BE any worse?

OBVS not. Well, maybe if he had been kidnapped by that EVIL NEMESIS in the underground lair I was talking about, but like THAT'S not going to happen because he's too busy trying to catch me to worry about a baby bird like Luca.

Which, like, WHY BOTHER, because it's clear I can stitch myself up ALL ON MY OWN.

So, I am back to having to think up brand new Plans A to C and it looks like I am going to have to either:

a) LIE to the girls, and say he TOTES ran away and I couldn't catch him and I think HE'S decided to join a circus.

c) FESS UP to the girls, only saying it's probably a good thing because that way at least he gets to play with some boys. Even if they are pigs.

c) Get Luca back before they find out and pretend NOTHING HAPPENED.

And the thing is, even though it is TOTES going to go wrong, because it involves me, Poppy, actually getting something right, I just KNOW it's got to be Plan C. I am going to HAVE to get Luca back before they find out. AND before Gale turns him into some kind of feathered flunky!

And to do that I have to absolutely NOT do anything POPPYISH, because if I've learned anything this week, it's that I get things WRONG almost ALL the time. Instead, I TOTES need to channel Willow and Stella and Dahlia.

I need to be CALM.

I need to be BRAVE.

And I need to be CLEVER.

And I also need to pack a disguise in case it all goes wrong and I end up hopping away after all.

2.30PM

Right, I'm pretty sure I've got everything I need:

1. Sunglasses (from Dahlia)
2. Lipstick (from Stella)
3. Giant hat (from Willow)

Lucky they were all out again. Without me. Probably rehearsing with the band. Or having another picnic. Or a milkshake and skateboarding party. Which I'm not even ONE BIT sad about. Well, OK, I am. But on the plus side it means they didn't notice me borrowing their kit. And I'll be back by dinner so they'll never even know I was missing. Plus I had this GENIUS idea just in case I'm not. I've TOTES made another me! I know, right? I used just a TEENSY-WEENSY bit of Dahlia's Double Trouble potion and PING – now there's another Poppy who can cover for me when I'm gone! OK, so she doesn't talk at all, and one of her eyes is wonky, and she's quite a bit shorter than me, but like they'd even NOTICE. And OK, it's KIND OF a prank, but it's in a good cause so it doesn't REALLY count. OBVS I have NO idea what I'll do with her when I get back. But I'll worry about that later. Right now all I can think about is Luca

and what that awful Bad Princess is doing to him right now.

I just wish I was doing this with the girls. When they're with me, I'm not worried about ANYTHING, because together we're unstoppable. But on my own, well, that's a different story. I might come across as just a LEEETTLE bit loud sometimes, but I feel like all I am is a whisper without my home birds. And if I get this wrong, I might never get to do anything with them again.

So, wish me luck, dear Diary. The next time I write in here, I might be living in exile on Planet Neuron. Which, like, I don't even know where that IS because I just made it up!

3.30PM

OK, so I'm not on Planet Neuron. I'm in Gale's castle, but it might as well be another planet because it's SO much farther away than I thought. Plus I forgot you have to navigate the SKANKY SWAMPS and the MAHOOSIVE

MOUNTAINS and, even worse, the PIGS PLAY PARK. Which isn't skanky or mahoosive but it IS hilarious and I thought I was going to EXPLODE laughing about a BAZILLION times when they kept falling off the see-saw which would have TOTES given the game away. Not that this is a game. This is serious. And scary. Scarier than I thought POSSIBLE. And definitely scarier than Planet Neuron, even if it wasn't made-up, and was actually infested by bird-eating mega-sharks. Because I've found Luca. And he's not tied up. Or handcuffed. Or glued to a barrel that's about to be rolled down a waterfall (the pigs have totes done that to each other before). It's WORSE.

He's ...

Oh I almost can't bear to write it ...

He's ...

Okay, strength, Poppy. Channel Stella.

He's ... DRESSED AS A BABY PRINCESS.

Which, like, I KNOW, right?!

He's got a dummy in his beak, and a pink bonnet, and Handsome Pig is rocking him in a cradle while Gale squawks a lullaby, which is SO not going to send him to sleep. I mean, she has a voice like a volcano erupting. Poor Luca. This is way worse than the time he got stuck halfway down a tube and had to be rocketed out with cold water.

Worse even than the time he tried some bubblegum and got his beak stuck together and couldn't make a sound for a whole HOUR.

I mean, this is the worst kind of worse possible. Which, what is that? Dahlia would know. Only Dahlia's not here. It's just me. And I'm twittering on about NOTHING when I should be concentrating on saving Luca or he's going to be wearing a nappy and getting burped before I can say 'Back to business'.

OK, so the plan is this: I'm going to wait until Gale goes off for her beauty sleep (she needs A LOT of that) and then I'll somehow distract Handsome Pig. All I need to do is work out how.

I mean, what would distract a vain, silly, Princess-obsessed pig?

A mirror?

A film contract?

A pair of diamond-encrusted underpants?

A princess?

OMG. That's IT! A PRINCESS. And not just ANY princess. But the one, the only, BAD princess. GALE.

I need to make another version of her. I KNEW I shouldn't have left the Double Trouble potion behind. Then I could just sprinkle some over Gale in her sleep and PING! Another annoying, brattish, bighead. Though actually the thought of that is, like, TERRIFYING. TWO Gales? I mean, one is way too many!

No, I'll have to do it the old-fashioned way and disguise myself. Though it's going to be

almost IMPOSSIBLE. I mean, I'm not exactly
Princess material, am I. Princesses are polite,
and neat, and never ever get into trouble.
Whereas I'm loud, messy and in a whole HEAP
of bother. Lucky I brought that lipstick with me.
And the sunglasses. And Willow's hat. Not that
I'm going to *wear* the hat. It's more what she
has hidden inside it. I've seen her pull an actual
rabbit out of it before. Fingers crossed she's got a
pink satin ballgown and a tiara!

4PM

OK, so NO pink satin ballgown or tiara but I DID
find:

1. Some cardboard and a pair of scissors.
2. Some gold paint.
3. A packet of jelly sweets.
4. Half a pineapple, a paintbrush and a packet of
   biscuits (that bird seriously needs to clear out
   her handbag!)

So, I TOTES don't need the last three, but I've made myself a gold crown with rubies (strawberry jellies) and emeralds (lime jellies) and sapphires (I don't even KNOW what fruit they're meant to be but they taste like soap) and I've borrowed a purple curtain I found in one of the spare bedrooms as a cape. It's not perfect: I've got gold paint stuck to half of my feathers and the cape is WAY too big and I keep falling over, but it's all I've got, and like Willow says: you've got to work with what you've got and make the best of a situation.

If she was here she'd be doing some special Save Luca dance by now. And Stella would be booby-trapping all the doors. And Dahlia would be building a getaway car from a sofa and a juice machine.

But they're not here. It's just me, Poppy, in a home-made disguise, about to persuade Handsome Pig he's TOTES in love with me so that he goes so GOOGLY-EYED he hands over the hostage and we can hightail it out of here before anyone even knows we're missing.

Easy-peasy. NOT!

I am SO winging it. But, like Stella says: 'What's the worst that could happen?'

I could end up getting kidnapped too and made to wear a BONNET?

I could get given to the pigs as some sort of EGGSPERIMENT? Which I would TOTES laugh at if I wasn't feeling ACTUALLY SICK.

5PM

Or, I could end up getting totally caught in the act of KISSING HANDSOME PIG. Which, like, EWWWWWWW. And also NOOOOOOOO. But mainly EWWWWWWW. I mean, it wouldn't have been QUITE so FANTABULOUSLY DISGUSTING if no one had seen me do it. But they DID.

I mean not the first time. The first time it was just me falling over the giant curtain cape and saying 'Oh, but Handsome Pig, I really do TOTES love you after all!' And wishing I hadn't broken Dahlia's love potion and had drunk it all instead so it wouldn't be so UNCONVINCING or

DISGUSTING. Only Handsome Pig was TOTES convinced (pigs really are THAT stupid) and gave me a huge, horrible, hog kiss right there and then, which was enough time for Luca to jump out of the cradle and into my bag.

Only just as I was about to make a fast getaway, claiming I need to get even MORE beauty sleep, he begged me for one last smacker. And I was so scared he'd notice Luca was missing that I did it. I kissed him RIGHT on his stinky snout. Which, like, I KNOW. On a scale of one to ten it was a ninety-nine. Like, totally worse than rolling in super-slime. Worse than accidentally eating a mouldy mulberry. Worse EVEN than kissing a frog. Which, like, I totes tried because Willow once said she'd heard it would turn into a handsome prince which it so DID NOT, it just croaked and jumped in the air. But who needs a prince anyway, right?

Certainly not one who's actually just a stinky, snorting PIG. Which, again, UGH.

But that's not the point. The point is, to make matters EVEN worse (which I didn't think was possible after snogging a hog) the kiss was RIGHT when Stella, Willow, Dahlia AND Gale all stormed in. Not EVEN joking.

Which means I am TOTES:

1. RED with embarrassment. Like, even redder than a cherry that's just eaten a bowl of tomato soup and then gone for a swim in a pool of strawberry jam.
2. Feeling SICKER than if I'd eaten the cherry, the tomato soup and the pool of strawberry jam.
3. In BIG TROUBLE.

Plus Gale is having a meltdown because she says Semolina (she means Luca, only apparently his name wasn't fancy enough) was her Best and ONLY Bird Friend and she was going to bring him up to be a PRINCE and now I've ruined her life as well as his because now he'll just be a boring NORMAL bird like the rest of us. I said I wished I WAS normal, but I'm pretty sure Stella was about to tell me I'm all SORTS of other things, like RECKLESS, and IRRESPONSIBLE and JUST PLAIN STUPID. Only Stella said that could wait until we got home. Which is where I am right now. Well, not ACTUAL home because Stella wouldn't let me sulk in my treehouse, she said I had to wait at Willow's while the others all went for a quiet word. Which means they're probably thinking up some even worse things to say to me RIGHT NOW.

So, goodbye, dear Diary. This is IT. I am about to be PUNISHED. And given that the last punishment was a whole week of not pranking, which was, like the WORST THING EVER, this one is going to be so MIND-BLOWINGLY BAD that I'll probably wish I had gone to Planet Neuron. Because, even though it doesn't exist, it HAS to be better than here.

7PM

So, THAT was weird. And, well, kind of good.

No, not just KIND OF good. ACTUALLY good.

No, not ACTUALLY good. TOTES good.

In fact, SO TOTES good I'd say it was the BEST THING EVER. Which, like, I KNOW!

I mean, it didn't start off so brilliantly. I had to explain Poppy 2 for a start and Dahlia was more than a TEENSY-WEENSY bit cross I'd borrowed the Double Trouble potion because she hasn't perfected it yet because after a while the doubles start to shrink and then they disappear altogether which she says is a design fault and Stella says is a massive relief. I asked if that was how they realised it wasn't ACTUALLY me, because the other Poppy had shrunk? Which made Dahlia laugh, which made me TOTES see red, and I said, 'Or was it because she did all the things you wanted me to do, like NOT SHOUT, or NOT PLAY TRICKS, or NOT BREAK things?'

Only Willow said, 'She was different, yes. But not in a good way.'

And Stella said, 'That's what made us realise how wrong we'd been. Because she DIDN'T shout, or play tricks or break things.'

And Dahlia said, 'Or make us laugh, or play us a twenty-minute drum solo when we're feeling down, or give us a TOTES amazing empty jam jar she'd found on the beach.'

And that's when I knew she really DID feel bad. Because there is NO WAY Dahlia would say 'TOTES' unless she really did like me.

Plus Willow gave me one of her hugs and tied this AMAZING scarf round my neck. You know, the one I said I didn't give two TWEETS about because it so OBVS wasn't for me. Only it turns out I did. And it was. Which, like, YAY!

And Stella said she had something to show me, only I had to shut my eyes. Which I did, only Willow put her hat over my head in case I peeked, which, like I SO wouldn't have. Well, I might. But it wouldn't have mattered because what I saw when I took the hat off was AMAZEBALLS!

It was my treehouse. But NOT the boring, tidy one I left behind – the cluttered, messy one just FULL of junk from the beach. Only Dahlia said, 'It's not junk, it's treasure, we know that now. Just like you are. A hundred and ten per cent.'

And I was so happy I thought I might cry. Which, like, would have been ALMOST as icky as kissing Handsome Pig. Unless you're Willow who cries when blades of grass get squished. Which, I'm not. And I told them. I said, 'I tried SO hard to be like all of you. I tried to be CALM like Willow, and BRAVE like Stella and CLEVER like Dahlia. But the thing is, I'm not. I'm just plain old Poppy.'

'But don't you get it?' said Stella. 'You ARE all those things. You're calm in a crisis, because you thought to pack a bag with things you might need. And you're clever. I mean, who else would have thought to dress up as Bad Princess to win over Handsome Pig's heart? And most of all you're brave. You KISSED A PIG. That's the bravest thing EVER.'

'Really?' I said.

'Really,' said Stella. 'So don't try to be anyone else. Be yourself. You're pretty special, Pops.'

'Super special,' said Willow.

'Like, TOTES,' said Dahlia. 'And SO much better than that new Poppy. I really have to work on that potion.'

'So where is she now?'

'Oh, she's birdsitting Luca. The wonky eye comes in handy for that. She can't take it off him. Wherever he wanders, so does the eye! It'll almost be a shame when she disappears.'

'I bet she doesn't prank though,' I said. 'And I won't either. I promise. I'm done with all that now. I've learned my lesson. You were right about it being about me. I just wanted you to like me, but instead the pranks always made you cross.'

'Not always,' said Stella.

'Only sometimes,' said Willow.

'Hardly ever,' said Dahlia. 'In fact, we'd quite like it if you went back to pranking as soon as possible. We want our old Poppy back.'

And EVEN THOUGH they all hugged me again then ... and EVEN THOUGH there is nothing more I like than a good, messy, hilarious prank ... and EVEN THOUGH I've thought up a brilliant one involving the book about bees, the red sock and a pot of peanut butter, I am TOTES NEVER going to prank again. Not at all. Not even a TEENSY-WEENSY trick.

8PM

Not until tomorrow anyway...
    Night, Diary.

DON'T MISS THE NEXT ADVENTURE...

STELLA RUNS AWAY!

Unbelievable! This is completely ridiculous!

I found a note outside my door that said, 'Good morning, Stella. Today we're going to rehearse at the top of the biggest tree on the island.'

You can't rehearse in a tree.

Like *duhhh*.

No. I'll try to keep a positive attitude here. Maybe Willow, with her artistic mindset, wants to try out some different places. And you do get nice views from a tree.

LATER

Well. I have no words to describe what happened. Still, I'll try to get the whole weird episode down in writing.

When I arrived at the base of the biggest tree on the island, I saw Poppy, Dahlia and Luca already on a big branch near the top.

'Hey, friends, I'm on my way up!' I called out, and then they all started acting really weird. They didn't look excited the way they normally do when they see a friend. They looked like they were hiding something.

'Oh, hi,' Dahlia said in a flat voice.

'Where's Willow?' I asked, once I had reached the top.

'Over there, asleep,' Poppy pointed down and gave an odd fake smile.

Willow's hat was way off at the edge of the forest.

'Let's wake her up. We've got band practice now,' I said.

But Dahlia had other ideas. 'Let Willow sleep if she's tired,' she said. 'We'll practise the parts where she's not needed.'

How lazy, I thought. 'OK, she can sleep. But only for a little while. Where are the instruments?' I asked, but Poppy was looking at the others and Dahlia was fidgeting with some leaves. Luca was pretending to be a leaf, hanging and swinging from a branch.

'The what?' Dahlia asked, as if she hadn't heard my question.

'The instruments!' I was starting to get irritated.

'Oh … yeah,' Dahlia said.

I saw Poppy nudge Dahlia. 'Tell her,' she whispered.

'Tell me what?' I asked.

Dahlia blushed. Finally, she said, 'The thing is, if you think about all the strains on a bird's health, like, if we practise every day, your feathers might fall out, and …' Dahlia explained with a strange expression on her face.

'Yeah, what Dahlia's trying to say is, shouldn't we take a day off?' Poppy asked, still smiling that weird smile, with her mouth open so wide that a fly actually flew in there and then flew back out, shaking its head.

'Willow, wake up! These guys up here are going on about taking a day off,' I shouted as I got down from the tree.

'Don't wake her up!' Poppy shrieked after me, but I didn't pay any attention, because night-time is for sleeping.

'Wake up!' I nudged the sleeping Willow ... but it wasn't Willow! It was just a heap of moss with a hat on top!

And it wasn't even Willow's hat – it was somebody else's.

'Where's Willow, and what's going on here?' I demanded.

Poppy cautiously came over to where I was standing.

'Oh, if only we knew. And if only we knew where the sun came from or why water is wet or why trees have leaves, and not birds that look like Luca,' she babbled.

'Let's call Willow on the speaky,' I said, but Dahlia, who had just come down out of the tree, butted in.

'The line's not working today. It's too cloudy,' she said.

'But there aren't any clouds,' I said.

'You see, there are extremely rare invisible clouds in the sky today,' Dahlia began.

'Yeah, that's it. Everybody knows that,' Poppy added.

'What are you talking about?' I shouted angrily.

'Ahem … ahem … cough, cough,' Dahlia coughed and went to lie down on the ground with her eyes closed.

'What's wrong with you?' I asked in alarm.

'I think I'm coming down with something,' Dahlia said weakly.

'I'll take Dahlia home to rest,' Poppy said brightly, and I thought I saw Dahlia wink at Poppy, but maybe it was just a symptom of her illness.

'I'll come too,' I said, but Poppy resisted.

'No, don't,' she said. 'It's better if the infection doesn't spread to everybody. You stay here with Luca.'

And then they were gone. I just stood there with Luca, feeling like a prat. I've never felt so dumb before. It's not often I am lost for words, but my friends' behaviour had been so weird that I somehow just froze.

Back home, I sat and thought about our band rehearsals over the past few days. There have been some strange things going on:
1. Our rehearsal times have been really weird.
2. Our rehearsal spaces have been really weird.
3. My friends have been acting really weird.

What's going on here? It might be because:
1. They don't like me anymore.
2. They want to be friends with each other, but not with me.

We just said that friendship oath recently. How can my best friends seem as weird as Gale all of a sudden? I shouldn't think about terrible things like that. Of course they're my friends.

I drank my evening cup of tea and took my speaky out from under the bed. I pressed the button and chirped into it.

'Yoo-hoo, any friends out there? It's me, Stella.'

Nobody seemed to be on the line.

'Hey, friends! It's Stella calling,' I added, and then the device crackled. I could hear some unclear voices coming through.

'Don't answer!'

'I pressed it by accident ... Shhh ...'

I could hear some odd noises and tapping.

'Luca, Poppy, Willow, Dahlia?' I called out, because along with the tapping I thought I could hear all their voices.

'Stella, it's Dahlia here. How's it going? I hope we won't get cut –'

The line was cut off.

Silence.

'Hello? Dahlia?' But there was no sound from the speaky. How weird. Was it broken? Maybe there was a problem on the line, causing the random sounds …

A LITTLE LATER

I woke up from a deep sleep to hear my name being called through the speaky.

'Stella! Stellaaaa!' Poppy called.

'Are you there, Stella?' Dahlia's voice asked.

I didn't feel like getting out of bed, because I'd been asleep and was feeling miserable.

'Is that S, is that T, is that E, is that L, is that L …' I heard Poppy joking into the speaky, but I switched it off and pulled the covers over my ears. I didn't feel like talking to them.

I went to sleep and had a nightmare about Gale. I had transformed into Gale's talking crown and could only say, 'Is that S, T, E, L, L, A, I, S, D, U, M, B?'

And then I woke up in a cold sweat.

AS SEEN IN THE APP

DON'T MISS
THE OTHER BOOKS IN THIS
EXCITING,
NEW SERIES!

STELLA, DAHLIA, POPPY, WILLOW AND LUCA:

BEST FRIENDS FOREVER... MOST OF THE TIME!

MASTER THE
SUPERPOWERS OF
THE FEARLESS FLOCK,
IN OVER 120
ACTION-PACKED
LEVELS!

FREE TO PLAY!

EGMONT

E2213